The Big Ballet Show

Adapted by Geof Smith

Based on the screenplay "Dora's Ballet Adventure" by Teri Weiss

Illustrated by John Loter and Brenda Goddard

 A GOLDEN BOOK • NEW YORK

randomhouse.com/kids
ISBN: 978-0-307-93094-1
Printed in the United States of America
10 9 8 7 6 5 4 3 2

It was the day of the big Dance Show. Dora and her friends were getting ready backstage. Everyone was very excited. They all loved to dance.

"Are you ready to start the show?" Boots asked Dora.

"Almost," she replied. "We're just waiting for the Delivery Duck to bring our dance slippers from the Dance School."

Suddenly, the Delivery Duck flew into the room with a box.

Dora quickly opened the box and looked inside. "Oh, no!" she cried. "These aren't dance slippers! These are scuba flippers! We can't dance in these."

Dora and Boots told the other dancers they would run to the Dance School and get the slippers.

"We'll be back in time to start the Dance Show," Dora said. Everyone wished her luck.

"How will we find the Dance School?"
Boots asked.

"Let's ask Map!" said Dora.

Map said that to reach the Dance School,
they had to go through Bunny Hop Hill and
Benny's Barn.

Dora and Boots ran and ran until they came
to Bunny Hop Hill. There was a door in the hill,
but it didn't have a knob.

"How are we going to open the door?"
Boots asked.

Luckily, a helpful bunny hopped up to them.

"You need to go through three doors to get through Bunny Hop Hill," the bunny said. "To open them, you have to play Follow the Bunny. Just do what I do!"

Dora and Boots hopped like the bunny to open the first door.

They shook their bunny tails to open the second door.

To open the third door, they wiggled their ears like the bunny.

Dora and Boots opened all the doors and
made it through Bunny Hop Hill. After thanking
the bunny, they ran to Benny's Barn.

"Hi, Benny," Dora said. "We need to pass through your barn to go to the Dance School and get our dance slippers."

"No problem, Dora," replied Benny. "And guess what? You're just in time for the Animal Dance Hoedown!

"To get through the barn, you have to dance like an animal," Benny said.

"Jump like a frog!

"Gallop like a horse!

"And flap your arms
like a chicken!"

"We made it through Benny's Barn," Dora
said. "Now we have to run to the Dance School
and get those slippers!"

Dora and Boots finally reached the Dance School—but the front gate was locked!

"How will we open the gate?" Boots asked.

"There must be a key to unlock it," Dora replied. "Let's try to find it."

Dora spotted some keys hanging from a branch. She was about to take them when Swiper jumped out from behind the tree. He wanted to swipe the keys!

"Swiper, no swiping!" Dora and Boots said.

"Oh, mannn!" Swiper said, and gave Dora the keys.

Dora opened the gate, went into the school, and found the box of dance slippers. But it was almost time for the Dance Show! How would she and Boots get back in time?

Suddenly, the Dance Train rolled by and offered them a ride!

The Dance Train raced quickly along the tracks. Dora and Boots were at the Dance Show in no time.

When they arrived with the box of slippers, the other dancers cheered. "¡Fantástico! Dora and Boots saved the Dance Show!"

Everyone danced beautifully, especially Dora.
She performed a special ballet piece to start
the show!

When the Dance Show was over, all the
friends and family in the audience applauded.
Benny gave Dora a bunch of colorful flowers.
Dora liked flowers, and she really liked dancing.
But most of all, she liked saving the day and
making her friends happy.